SMITTEN

WITH CANDY CANES

A SWEET ROMANTIC COMEDY

SET IN FINLAND

ELLEN JACOBSON

Large Print ISBN: 978-1-951495-31-2
Print ISBN: 978-1-951495-30-5
Digital ISBN: 978-1-951495-29-9

Editor: By the Book Editing
Cover Design: Melody Jeffries Design

First Printing: February 2022

Published by: Ellen Jacobson
www.ellenjacobsonauthor.com

For Santa Claus and all of his elves.

Thanks for all the awesome presents
over the years!

CONTENTS

CHAPTER 1
UNLUCKY NUMBER THIRTEEN

As I board the plane, I remind myself that I'm not a superstitious kind of girl.

Well, except when it comes to hedgehogs. Why anyone thinks they're adorable is beyond me. The creatures have spines, people, spines. If that's not a dead giveaway that they're bad news, I don't know what is.

Need more convincing about hedgehogs? Ask me about the time a certain photographer thought it would be funny if . . .

Actually, let's not talk about that. The

last thing I need to be reminded of is how Max Guerrero made me look like an idiot.

Stop thinking about that jerk, Zoe. Focus on getting to your seat without spilling your peppermint mocha.

Taking a deep breath, I tighten my grip on my coffee cup. As I inch down the aisle, I scan the row numbers, looking for my seat. When I reach row thirteen, my stomach twists into knots. I can't figure out what's going on. Thirteen is just a number. I don't buy into that mumbo-jumbo that the number thirteen is unlucky. So why am I so anxious? Why do I have this feeling that something horrible is about to happen?

"Lady, are you gonna take your seat?"

I smile apologetically at the man behind me, then squeeze into the aisle seat. Balancing my cup in one hand, I set my purse on the seat next to me. Once I'm settled, I take a cautious sip of my mocha and end up burning the tip of my tongue. Removing the lid to cool it down, I smile at the sight of crushed up candy cane pieces nestled on top of whipped cream. You can keep your gingerbread and eggnog lattes. Nothing says Christmas like peppermint to me.

Of course, what really says Christmas is my mom's candy cane cheesecake, but I won't be getting any this year. My family is back in California, while I'm heading to Finland to write a travel article on Santa's Village. My mom and sister were understanding. This is a great assignment, but still, Christmas won't be the same without them.

A young boy, maybe five or six years old, pops his head over the seat in front of me, distracting me from my thoughts of working over Christmas. He bounces up and down on his mother's lap, clutching a small toy truck in one hand. Then he giggles and flings the toy in my direction.

Guess where it lands. Yep, in my

mocha. I wipe whipped cream out of my eyes, then groan when I look down at my coat. What used to be a cute pink puffer jacket is now a brown splotchy mess.

"Gimme my truck," the boy says.

"Say 'please,' Christopher," his mother prompts automatically, unaware of what damage her son's truck has done.

The boy holds out his hand. "Gimme my truck, *please.*"

I fish the toy out of my cup, then wipe it off with a napkin. Christopher grins when I hand it to him, even remembering to say thank you. After shoving the cup into the seat back pocket, I try to remove the mocha stains from my coat. This is no job for a couple of crumpled up napkins. It's hopeless. What I need to do is wash it out with water, but people are still boarding. There's no way I'll be able to get to the bathroom.

As I take off my jacket, I glance up at

top of my head. I give the little boy a warning look, then press the phone back to my ear. "Since we don't have a photographer, what do you want to do about pictures? I guess I can always take some on my phone."

"Yeah, that's not a good idea," she says. "I've seen your Instagram account. What is with your thumbs? They're in every single picture."

"They're little ego-maniacs, trying to steal the limelight. Seriously, what do you want to do about pictures?"

"Well, I have arranged for another photographer." Nicole clears her throat. "I'm not sure how to tell you this, but—"

"Hang on a sec," I tell her as a commotion at the front of the plane distracts me. Leaning into the aisle, I see a man help an older woman place her suitcase into the overhead bin. His back is turned to me, but there's something familiar about his tall athletic frame, his broad shoulders, and his dark curly hair. When he turns, I gasp.

Actually, maybe it was less of a gasp and more of a subdued shriek. I'm sitting in the middle of a crowded plane, so it's not like I'd yell at the top of my lungs. But a subdued shriek? Well, that seems appropriate given who I just saw. Turns out the number thirteen really is unlucky.

"Is everything okay, Zoe?" Nicole asks.

"No, not really," I say, enunciating each word. "Want to tell me why Max Guerrero is on my flight?"

"You need a photographer and Max was available." Nicole laughs nervously. "It's better than thumbs in all the pictures."

I scowl. "I'd rather cuddle up with a hedgehog than work with that man."

"But hedgehogs freak you out," she says.

"Exactly."

"Hmm, fear of hedgehogs. I think

that's called skatzochoirophobia."

"Did your friend, Ginny, tell you that?" I ask.

"Uh-huh. You know how I've been trying to get her to come work for the magazine. But her fear of flying makes things more complicated."

"Yeah, I can see how that would be a problem." I take a sip of my mocha, then add, "I'm glad I'm only afraid of hedgehogs."

"That's not entirely true. You're afraid of Max."

"Afraid of Max? Me? You're joking."

"Sorry, I stand corrected. You're scared of your *feelings* for Max. I heard what happened between the two of you in Germany."

"It was one kiss," I say. "One, horrible, awful kiss. Thankfully, we haven't worked together since."

I suspect the tone of my voice was a bit shrill. I might have even let out another one of those subdued shrieks because it seems like everyone on the plane is looking at me.

Everyone, that is, except Max. He's too busy standing in the aisle flirting with a flight attendant. She's twirling a curl of hair around one of her fingers while he whispers something in her ear.

I grin as a voice over the speakers interrupts their little romantic moment.

"Ladies and gentlemen, this is your captain speaking. I apologize for the delay. Please take your seats at this time for departure. Flying time from London to Finland is three hours and thirty-six minutes. If we're lucky, we might spot Santa Claus taking his reindeer out for a test flight before the big day."

All the kids on board, plus some of the adults, start cheering at the mention of Santa. I get how spending Christmas in Santa's Village would be the perfect family vacation, but for someone like me, in their twenties without children, I just didn't get it.

"Zoe Randolph, what a pleasant surprise." I look up and see Max towering over me, a cocky grin on his face. "Nicole didn't tell me we'd be working together."

"Oh, come off it," I tell him. "You knew about this."

"Okay, I did." He shrugs, then points at the window seat. "Can I have the aisle seat? I have long legs."

I arch an eyebrow. "I do too."

"Funny, I never noticed."

The flight attendant sashays down the aisle. She places her hand on Max's arm, bats her eyelashes, and says, "Sir, please take your seat."

"Sure thing, Chanel."

As he winks at her, I roll my eyes. This chick might be named Chanel, but her perfume doesn't smell anything like those classic scents. Instead, her fragrance is a cross between bubblegum and doggy doo-doo—

definitely not a winning combination.

Why would Max be interested in someone like Chanel? Oh, yeah, he flirts with every woman, no matter what kind of perfume they wear.

I stand and indicate the window seat. He looks me up and down slowly, then says, "You do have long legs."

After we're seated and buckled in, he tosses me a candy cane. "Merry Christmas."

I wrinkle my nose and toss it back. "I don't like candy canes."

Okay, we both know that's not exactly the truth. I adore candy canes. Candy cane cheesecake, candy cane cookies, candy cane fudge . . . you get the idea. But there's no way I'm telling Max about my obsession.

"I thought everybody liked candy canes," Max says.

"Not this girl," I say. "Why don't you give it to that flight attendant, Chanel?"

"Actually, she gave it to me."

"Let me see if I've got this right," I say, shaking my head. "You're trying to re-gift a candy cane?"

"Lighten up, Zoe. It's just a piece of candy. It's not like it means anything." Max offers it to the little boy sitting in front of us. Then he leans back and gives me a lazy smile. "You're not going to try to kiss me on this trip like you did in Germany, are you?"

I fling my in-flight magazine at him, then jam my earbuds in and turn up the volume on my phone. While I listen to Eartha Kitt sing *Santa Baby*, I remind myself that I'm a professional. I'm flying to Finland to do a job. I can put up with Max Guerrero for a week. Right?

* * *

I have never been so relieved to close a hotel room door in my life.

Okay, to be honest, I slammed it. Right in Max's smug little face.

Actually, is it relief that I feel? No, that doesn't quite describe it. Satisfying? Maybe. Rewarding? Kind of. Pleasurable? Hmm . . pleasurable . . .

No, no, no! Max Guerrero and the word "pleasurable" are two things that do not go together. Ever. Stop thinking about how your body tingled when his hand brushed against yours on the airplane. Stop thinking about how your stomach did flip-flops when his dark brown eyes held your gaze for a moment too long. Just stop it.

I go into the bathroom and splash cool water on my face. As I dab my face with a hand towel, I analyze how I'm feeling. Being able to label your emotions is important. At least that's what the in-flight magazine said.

I straighten my shoulders and look at myself in the mirror. I know exactly how I feel about Max. Indifference with a splash of disdain.

With that all cleared up, I get busy

unpacking my suitcase. Then I collapse onto the bed and take in my surroundings. Birch paneled walls, muted colors, sheepskin rugs, and large windows looking out at snow-covered trees. I'm not sure how you'd describe the decor—contemporary Scandinavian, perhaps?—but what I do know is that it's snug, comfortable, and so relaxing I drift off to sleep.

A banging on the door wakes me up, interrupting a strange dream about Max dressed up as Santa Claus and surrounded by hedgehogs in elf costumes. It's kind of funny because Max *hates* wearing costumes. At the annual company Halloween party, he's the only person who doesn't dress up.

I check the time on my phone. Crap. I'm late. Jumping out of bed, I run my fingers through my snarled hair. Knowing who's on the other side, I take a deep breath before yanking the door open.

"Max, what a lovely surprise," I say. News flash: it isn't.

"We're late." Max asks, pushing past me. "The welcome dinner started five minutes ago."

"Oh, wow. Five whole minutes. How will we ever live down the shame?"

Max doesn't seem to notice my sarcastic tone. He taps his watch. "Six minutes now. This is why I didn't want to work with you again."

I put my hands on my hips. "And you think I want to work with you? Fat chance."

"Let's find you something to wear," Max says as he opens my closet.

"Hey, get out of there," I say. "In fact, get out of my room. I know how to dress myself."

Shaking his head, he says, "I'm not leaving here. If I do, by the time you get downstairs, we'll already be on dessert."

Yanking a dress off a hanger, I storm into the bathroom to change. I poke my head out and glare at Max. "I'll meet you in the lobby." Then I slam the door right in his smug little face again. Boy, did that ever feel good.

* * *

When I walk into the lobby, Max gives a low whistle. "You clean up well."

I start to smile, wondering what's caused this change of heart. Why is he being nice to me? Maybe it's my dress. Based on the way he's looking at me, I think he's noticed how the full skirt and nipped-in waist flatters my curvy figure. Not that I wore it for him. No siree, wasn't even thinking about him when I put it on.

My smile broadens. Then Max taps his watch impatiently and the spell is broken.

Scowling, I follow him into the dining room set aside for our group.

A middle-aged woman with strawberry

blonde hair, a smattering of freckles, and an infectious grin welcomes me. "I'm Lumi, your tour director."

"Lumi means 'snow' in Finnish, doesn't it?" I ask.

"Oh, you speak Finnish." Lumi beams at me, then proceeds to rattle something off, presumably in Finnish.

I hold up my hands. "Uh, no. I only know a few words, like how to say please and thank you. And since we're in Santa's Village, surrounded by snow, I thought that might be useful too."

"Show-off," Max whispers.

"It's called research," I whisper back.

Lumi looks back and forth at the two of us, then says, "Ah, you two are, how do you say it, lovebirds?"

My face reddens. "Um, we're not—"

Max puts his arm around my shoulders, interrupting me. "Lovebirds, that's correct. Sorry for being late. It won't happen again," he says to Lumi. Then he turns to me. "Right, babe?"

"It's fine," Lumi says. "We are waiting for . . . Oh, there they are now."

As Lumi scoots off to greet the new arrivals, I pull away from Max. "Lovebirds? What's going on?"

He shrugs. "She thinks we're a couple."

"And you didn't correct her misconception?"

"Nah, it's more fun this way." Max grins. "Besides, this is payback for Germany."

I stamp my foot. "For the last time, the only reason I kissed you was as a favor for a friend."

"Sure, a favor," he says dryly. "Well, now I need a favor. Pretend to be my girlfriend while we're on this trip."

I roll my eyes. "Yeah, right."

"No, I'm serious. Pretend to be my girlfriend."

I can't imagine he's actually being serious. "Listen, I faked liking you for five minutes in Germany. Maybe ten minutes top. Faking it for a week? Please, I'm not that good of an actress. Besides, even if I was, no one would buy it."

"Why not?"

"Because . . ." I think for a moment, then say triumphantly, "We have separate rooms. If we were a couple, wouldn't we be sharing a room?"

Max puts his hand on his chest in mock horror. "Sharing a room with a girl? What kind of guy do you think I am?"

Before I can tell him, Lumi calls for everyone's attention. "Please help yourself to some glögi. Glögi is a traditional Finnish mulled wine made with orange zest, cloves, cinnamon, cardamom, and ginger root. It's served over the holidays."

As a server hands each of us a glass, Max whispers in my ear. "Just play along, okay? Then I'll owe you."

"Owe me what?"

"Ladies' choice."

I take a sip of glögi and consider my options. After a few moments, the perfect idea comes to me. One that's bound to embarrass Max to no end. I hold out my hand and grin. "It's a deal . . . babe."

CHAPTER 2
A DEAL'S A DEAL

Have you ever had an awkward handshake? We all have, haven't we? Like the ones where the other person tries to project confidence by crushing all the bones in your hand. (Top tip: When dealing with a bone crusher, casually ask if they have any suggestions for how to cure the rash on your hand. That'll end the handshake quickly.)

The opposite is almost as bad—the person who gives you a quick, limp handshake. Either they're riddled with insecurities or they just overheard you talk about the rash on your hand and want to minimize contact with you.

Of course, no one likes a soggy handshake. It either means that the other person is nervous or they recently applied some rash cream. Either way, have a tissue at the ready to discreetly wipe your hands.

All of these thoughts are going through my head while Max stares at my outstretched hand for what seems like forever. What's going on? Why is he hesitating? Is he concerned that I have some sort of contagious rash? What is wrong with me? Why do I keep thinking about rashes?

Finally, he takes my hand in his. I expect the brief clasping of hands followed by a normal release. Instead, he lightly caresses my hand, tracing his thumb along the back of it. "Tell me, Zoe, what will I owe you?"

"You'll see," I say, my voice cracking slightly. Stupid voice.

He arches an eyebrow. "I don't have that kind of patience. You have to tell me before we agree."

Max starts to pull his hand away but I increase my grip. Not in a bone-crushing sort of way. Because, trust me, I'm not feeling at all confident in this particular moment. I hold his gaze and say, "Nope, no can do. See, we're already shaking hands. We have an agreement."

I glance down horrified, realizing it's now me caressing Max's hand. Shuddering, I try to end the handshake. Max laughs—a deep throaty laugh that makes me tingle from head to toe—then pulls me toward him. I can't tell who's caressing whose hand now. Maybe we both are.

"Okay, but don't forget your end of the deal," he says softly. "Convince everyone that you're my girlfriend."

I shrug. "I can do that. I'm a pretty good actress. I had you fooled in Germany, didn't I?"

Is it my imagination or did Max's eyes turn steely for a moment? Nope, must be my imagination. He's giving me his usual cheeky grin. As he releases my hand, he says, "We can talk about who fooled who in Germany some other time. What you need to focus on now is fooling everyone here that we're an item." He points at a stunning redhead across the room. "Especially her."

"Oh, Max, what have you gotten yourself into?" I ask dryly.

* * *

Lumi asks for everyone's attention before Max has a chance to tell me what's going on between him and the redhead.

Once everyone quiets down, Lumi says, "Before I talk you through the activities we have planned during your stay at Santa's Village, why don't we go around the room and introduce ourselves?"

Our fellow travelers are an interesting mix. A sweet retired couple, a professor of Nordic studies and her husband, a military couple based in Germany, and a few families with kids of varying ages. One of those kids just happens to be Christopher, the little boy who was seated in front of me on the plane.

But it's the two girls who are doing a year abroad at the University of Helsinki who get my attention. Georgia is tall and willowy with those chiseled facial features that can pull off a pixie cut. Her friend, Barbie, is a petite curvy girl with a tousled mane of red hair. Yes, that redhead. Could she make it any more obvious that she has the hots for Max?

When Lumi turns to us, she tells the group that we work for a travel magazine. "Zoe and Max are here to do a story about what it's like to spend Christmas in Santa's Village."

The redhead waves her hand at Max. "You can interview me, if you want."

Max puts his arm around my waist. "My girlfriend is the writer. I just take the pictures."

"Even better," she purrs. "I'd love to do a photo shoot with you."

Oh, gag me. I'm sure her idea of a photo shoot with Max isn't exactly PG-rated.

Max shifts uncomfortably. He looks relieved when Lumi launches into an overview of our itinerary.

"We have an exciting week planned for you. Tomorrow, we're going to go dog sledding."

One of the kids pipes up. "Can we pet the dogs?"

"Of course. We'll have a chance to visit the husky kennels," Lumi says. "Then after dinner tomorrow, we're going to do an Arctic Circle crossing ceremony. Everyone will get a certificate presented by one of Santa's elves."

"Are you on Santa's naughty or nice list?" Max whispers to me. When I elbow him and tell him to shush, he says, "Based on that, I'm going to guess you're on the naughty one."

Lumi answers another husky-related question, then tells the group that she has a special treat lined up for us on Wednesday. "We'll be having dinner at the Ice Lodge. Some of you will be staying overnight too."

When Lumi indicates that Max and I will be among those spending the night in a hotel made entirely of ice, Max whispers, "Brr. That sounds cold. We'll have to snuggle up to keep warm."

I elbow him again. "Separate rooms, remember?"

"On Thursday, we'll go on a snowmobile expedition, and, on Friday, we're going to visit a reindeer farm and then go for a sleigh ride," Lumi says.

Christopher hops up and down. "Will we see Rudolph?"

"I think Rudolph will be busy." Lumi smiles. "But you will get to see Santa Claus on Christmas Eve. And then everyone flies home on Christmas Day after lunch."

Max gives me a mischievous grin and says loudly, "Aren't you scared of reindeer, babe?"

The rest of the group looks at me, and I shake my head.

"Oh, wait," Max says. "It's hedgehogs that freak you out."

"You know with the way your hair is sticking up, you kind of look like a hedgehog," I say.

Max scowls and runs his fingers through his hair, making it even more unruly. To be honest, it makes him look kind of adorable in an odd sort of way.

Apparently, Barbie thinks so too. She sidles over to Max and places her hand on his arm. "I have some styling products up in my room. Maybe after dinner, we could try some out."

Is "styling products" the latest code for you-know-what? It has to be because based on how she's looking Max over, I'm pretty sure she has more in mind than just taming his unruly locks.

Let's see, I have two options here— watch Max squirm some more or earn myself an Oscar for actress of the year. I opt for the latter. After all, we made a deal. I make it through this trip pretending to be Max's girlfriend and then he has to . . . well, you'll just have to wait and see what's going to happen. I promise it'll be worth it.

I loop my arm through Max's and plaster a smile on my face. "Sorry, I'm the only one who gets to style my boyfriend's hair."

The redhead shoots me a look that tells me she isn't going to give up that easy.

Game on, princess.

* * *

After dinner, I corner Max in the lobby. "Okay, spill. Why are you trying to convince Barbie that we're a couple?"

Max slumps into one of the armchairs by the fireplace. "Well, it's kind of embarrassing."

Sitting in the chair next to him, I rub my hands together. Max and an embarrassing story—this should be good. "Go on."

"Well, after our assignment in Germany, Nicole sent me to do a photo shoot in Sri Lanka. Let's just say that one of the guests on the tour took a fancy to me." When I shoot Max a glance, he holds up his hands. "I didn't do anything inappropriate. I was just being nice to her, like I'm nice to everyone."

"Uh-huh. Could it be that you were flirting with her?"

Max rubs the dark stubble on his chin.

"Maybe. But that's all it was, just flirting."

"So, what else is new? You flirt all the time."

"Turns out she had a boyfriend. He didn't join the tour group until later . . . and he got the wrong idea about the two of us." Max stares at the flames flickering in the fireplace for a moment, then says. "In my defense, she never told me about her boyfriend."

"Okay, so a jealous boyfriend. Big deal. What does this have to do with Barbie?"

"I met her while I was waiting at the check-in desk. I didn't realize at the time that she was going to be on this tour and—"

"Let me guess, you flirted with her."

"I prefer to think of it as being nice."

"Whatever," I say. "But what's the big deal? Why are you pretending that we're together?"

"Because Nicole would fire me if she thought I was hitting on one of the tour guests."

I arch an eyebrow. "Nicole said that?"

"In so many words. That girl from Sri Lanka, her boyfriend called Nicole to complain about me." Max spreads his hands out in front of him. "I can't afford to have any more misunderstandings. When I was waiting for you in the lobby, I realized that Barbie was part of this tour group and when Lumi said that we looked like lovebirds, well . . ."

When Max stares at the carpet, I finish his thought. "And that's when you decided you needed a fake girlfriend."

"You're still going to go through with it, right?" Max asks.

I nod. "A deal's a deal."

CHAPTER 3
SNOW ANGELS

The next morning, the shuttle bus picks the group up at the hotel to take us dog sledding. Max and I grab a seat near the front. I smile as Christopher and his mother board the bus. He bounces down the aisle dragging a large stuffed reindeer behind him. She looks like there isn't enough caffeine in the world to be able to cope with her son's energy level.

After the rest of the group takes their seats, Lumi boards the bus, a clipboard in her hands. "Do we have everyone?"

"Barbie and Georgia aren't here," the Nordic studies professor says from the back of the bus.

"Oh, isn't that a shame," I mutter under my breath.

"They must be running late. We'll give them a few minutes," Lumi says pleasantly.

"You snooze, you lose, don't you think?" I say to Max.

"You're one to talk," he says to me. "The only reason you made the bus on time is because I banged on your door."

I lean over and say quietly, "Well, you're the one who wants to avoid Barbie, not me. I would think you'd be happy if we left her behind."

Max shrugs. "Doesn't matter to me."

"If they don't show, then we don't have to pretend to be a couple."

"That's not the deal we made."

As Max grabs my hand and presses it to his lips, the retired couple says something about young love. I snatch my hand away.

Christopher yells from the back of the bus, "When are we going to see the huskies?" The other kids chime in, "Huskies, huskies, huskies!"

Lumi furrows her brow, then nods to the driver. As he puts the bus in gear, I see Barbie and Georgia running up.

As they board, Georgia apologizes to the group. "Sorry we're late. Barbie couldn't find her cell phone."

Barbie doesn't seem apologetic at all. She rests her hand on Max's shoulder and smiles at him. "I needed my phone to take pictures. You understand, don't you?"

Lumi motions to the rear of the bus. "Please take your seats."

Georgia makes her way down the aisle, but Barbie looks like she wants to sit on Max's lap, not with her friend.

"Your seat," Lumi says impatiently.

This time Barbie gets the hint, and we

finally depart.

* * *

When we get to our destination, the sound of dogs howling greets us. "They're excited you're here," Lumi says, before introducing us to the owners of the dog park—Timo and his wife, Eevi.

"We have one hundred and seven dogs here. Mostly Siberian huskies, but we also have Alaskan huskies, and Alaskan malamutes," Timo says. "These are hardy working dogs who can withstand cold and they love nothing more than to run."

While Timo tells us about this history of dog sledding in Finland, I can't help but smile at Barbie.

No, it's not because I've suddenly become fond of the girl. It's because she's wearing the most ridiculous outfit —a tight low-cut top (perfect for showing off her considerable assets), a thin down vest (left unzipped), ripped jeans (perfect for getting frostbite on her exposed skin), and high-heeled shoes (awesome for walking through the snow). Her only concession to the weather is a pair of gloves.

As Barbie wraps her arms around herself, shivering, Timo shakes his head. He says something to his wife, who rushes off. A few minutes later, Eevi returns with a pair of boots and a florescent orange snowsuit. She offers them to Barbie. The redhead scowls, but the cold must be getting to her because she dons the outfit.

When Max takes a picture of Barbie, she shrieks. "Delete that. I look awful."

"You look fine," he says.

Trust me, she doesn't look fine. The snowsuit is way too big for her and the orange color clashes with her hair. The only thing that looks cute are the embroidered felt boots. I wouldn't mind having a pair myself.

Barbie takes Max's comment as encouragement. "Do you really think so?"

I roll my eyes as she makes her way over to us. I think she's trying to do some sort of sexy sashay sort of walk. Instead, she looks like a demented pumpkin in her over-sized snowsuit as she shuffles through the snow.

"Uh, sure," Max says, inching backwards.

"Really?" she coos, continuing to shuffle toward him.

Enough already. I step in between the advancing pumpkin and Max. "Guys, pay attention. Timo is explaining what we're going to do."

Barbie looks miffed. Max shoots me a grateful glance.

Timo points at a wooden sled. "One person will stand at the back and steer. The other person will ride. We will stop halfway around the course so that you can switch places if you want. Everyone will go slow at first until you get the hang of steering, then we'll speed up."

Eevi assigns everyone a sled. Max and I are shown to the one at the rear.

"They're so cute." I bend down to pet the enthusiastic dogs who will be pulling our sled.

"The lead dog's name is Into," Eevi says. "It means 'eagerness.'"

Max laughs. "Seems appropriate. He seems eager to get going."

After Eevi shows us how to operate the sled, Max says to me, "Ladies, first."

"First for what? Driving or sitting?"

"Your choice."

"I'll drive," I say. "How hard can it be?"

The dogs are anxious to get going, especially Into, and it's only the fact that the sled is tied to a post that we don't just tear off across the snow.

Timo gives the signal and we take off. He's driving the lead sled, with Christopher and his mom snuggled under blankets in the front. Barbie and Georgia are in the next sled. Fortunately, three other sleds are between Barbie and us because otherwise I might risk being blinded by her orange snowsuit.

After a few minutes, I start to get the hang of steering the sled. Timo turns his head to survey the sleds behind him, then nods approvingly. He picks up speed and the rest of us follow suit. Gliding through the snow on a sled being pulled by dogs is an absolutely exhilarating feeling.

When Max twists his head and grins at me, I know he feels exactly the same way. "You're a natural," he says, holding up his phone to film me.

"The dogs make it easy," I say. "They're used to dealing with tourists like us. They're only pretending we're in charge."

"Hey, what's going on?" Max asks as our sled jerks to the left. "You're getting awfully close to the edge of the track."

"It isn't me," I say, trying to steer the sled back on course.

Into barks insistently, pulling the sled further and further to the left. Then he suddenly comes to a halt. Frightened our sled is going to crash into the dogs, I frantically press the brake, trying to slow down our forward momentum. The other dogs yelp, and get tangled up in each other. I gasp as the sled swerves up the embankment of snow, then tips over, causing Max and I to spill to the ground.

"Are you okay?" we both ask at the same time, our faces inches away from each other. Then we smile as we both say "fine" in unison.

I should feel cold lying in the snow, but I don't. The way Max is looking at me is making me feel like I'm melting from the inside out. My skin is burning, and it's not because of the bright sun. Why is this man having this effect on me? If I lay here much longer, I'm afraid the snow will turn into a puddle of water from my body heat.

"We should check on the dogs," Max says after a beat.

As he helps me to my feet, I giggle. "I think I know why we stopped. Someone was eager to take a bathroom break."

Into finishes his business, then looks at us like we're supposed to know what to do next.

Max scratches his chin. "Do you see the others?"

"No, they've gone around that bend. I wonder if they even know we aren't behind them?"

"Well, I guess we should try to untangle these guys," Max suggests.

Have you ever tried to untangle five squirming dogs? It's not easy. In their excitement, they keep running around in circles, tangling themselves up even more. My foot gets caught up in one of the leads, and I end up back on the ground, this time, not next to Max, but instead with an enthusiastic dog kissing my face.

Max grins. "I think you're getting a husky hug."

After he convinces the dog to get off me and untangles the lead wrapped around my ankle, I stretch out my arms and legs and make a snow angel.

"Having fun?" Max asks me.

"I grew up in southern California." I stand and wipe off my pants. "We never got up to the mountains to see the snow so I never got a chance to make snow angels or have snowball fights when I was a kid."

"So, you're making up for lost time?"

"Uh-huh. You should try it."

"Help me with the dogs, then I will."

After we get the dogs organized, I hold onto them firmly while Max rights the sled. I nod over at the snow bank. "Go on."

The mischievous look on Max's face

as he plops backwards reminds me of Christopher. I love how Max doesn't care how silly he looks as he spreads his arms and legs. My ex, Carl, would have never done anything like this. One time, I tried to get him to go on the merry-go-round at the local playground and he scoffed. "Those are for children, Zoe."

It wasn't long after that I broke up with him. Who wants to be with a guy who thinks merry-go-rounds are just for kids?

"Earth to Zoe," Max says, interrupting my thoughts.

"Do you like merry-go-rounds?" I ask him.

"Who doesn't? Although, the monkey bars are my favorite."

I feel something bubble up inside me, something I can't quite place. Quickly averting my eyes, I look down and compare our angels. We look cute in the snow, side by side. Then I shake my head. But in real life, we're a complete mismatch.

"We should probably head back," I say. "Why don't you drive this time?"

* * *

Thankfully, we make it back to the dog park without any further incident. Timo checks to make sure the dogs and sled are okay, then tells us to join the rest of the group at the kennels to see the puppies.

Despite how utterly adorable the pups are, I feel uncomfortable around Max. I think he feels the same way. Something happened during our dog sled ride, something neither of us wanted. The rest of our time at the dog park is awkward and the ride back to the hotel is subdued.

When we get to the lobby, I head to my room. As I rush up the stairs, I turn, half-expecting to see Max following me. It bothers me that I'm disappointed he's not. Is that because I want the chance to slam the door in his face again? Or is it because I want to kiss him again?

* * *

I feel better after a nap. All those feelings about Max were probably due to being at Santa's Village. It's Christmas-time. I'm missing my family and I'm sublimating my feelings onto Max. Or something like that. It's been a long time since my Psych 101 course in college.

I bundle up in my coffee-stained parka, wrap my mint-green scarf around my neck, and grab my matching mittens and hat. It's going to be cold at the Arctic Circle crossing ceremony. I can hardly wait to see if Barbie opts for high heels and ripped jeans again.

When I reach the meeting point outside a cafe, Max says, "You're late again."

Yep, we're back to our usual routine. I pull my phone out of my pocket and hold it up to him. "I'm exactly three minutes late. Three."

"Impressive. You can count to three. And you didn't even have to take off your mittens to use your fingers."

This is why I don't like this man—he's downright rude to me. That's how I know he's not my type whatsoever. The man is a natural smooth-talking flirt, constantly handing out compliments. All the ladies in the group just love him. Especially Barbie. I wonder why I never get the same treatment.

Lumi tries to get everyone's attention. When Barbie and Georgia finally get the hint and stop having a conversation about which of their professors is the cutest, Lumi points at a series of snow-covered pillars. Each one is topped with a lantern and they're all connected by a string of Christmas lights. "This line marks the southernmost latitude where the sun can stay below or above the horizon for twenty-four hours. In the summer, we call this the Midnight Sun, and in the winter, it is referred to as the Polar Night."

Lumi stretches her arms out. "I would like all of you to line up on the southern side. Now close your eyes and, on the count of three, step forward."

We all follow Lumi's instructions. When we open our eyes, she claps her hands. "Congratulations, you have now all officially crossed the Arctic Circle."

I glance to my right to smile at Max— after all, we're still pretending that we're a couple—but realize he isn't there. Chewing on my bottom lip, I look around for him, finally spotting him taking pictures of the group.

When he finishes he walks toward me. "I got some great shots of you. Did you know that when you close your eyes, you wrinkle your nose?"

As he shows the pictures to me, I feel

myself shivering.

"Are you cold, babe?" Max asks, playing up the role of the solicitous boyfriend to the hilt. "Why don't I get us some hot chocolate?"

I give him my best adoring gaze. "That would be great. Thanks, babe."

While Max goes into the cafe to get our beverages, Lumi approaches with one of Santa's elves. When the elf hands me a certificate embossed with a red wax stamp, Lumi says, "This is the proof of your crossing."

"What about Max?" I say. "Doesn't he get a certificate?"

"He was taking pictures when we did the official crossing, but I'm sure we can arrange something," Lumi says.

I turn when I hear Barbie's voice behind me. "I can do the crossing with him again. I wouldn't want him to have to do it alone."

What are we in high school? Is this like not being able to go to the bathroom by yourself?

"Uh, he's a big boy," I say. "I think Max can walk across a line without an escort."

"What's going on?" Max asks as he walks up to us.

"Oh you brought hot chocolate," Barbie says. "How sweet."

"I think that's for me," I say, taking both cups from him.

Barbie shrugs, then grabs Max's hand. "Come on, you need to do the crossing to get your certificate."

I try to take a sip from one of the cups, but it's too hot. These cups must have incredible insulation—it's freezing out here. You would have thought the short walk from the cafe to here would have cooled them down.

Setting both cups down on a bench, I remove my mittens so that I can pry the lid off one of them. I blow on the hot chocolate for a moment, then take a sip. Then I groan with pleasure. There's no better combination than rich dark chocolate and peppermint.

As I take another sip, Max walks back, a certificate in hand. He grabs the other cup from the bench. After he takes a drink, he says, "I think you got mine by mistake. I got a plain one for you because I know you hate anything with peppermint."

My brow furrows. I want nothing more than to keep drinking the delicious minty hot chocolate in my hand. "Um, I already had some of this one. Guess I'll have to suffer through drinking the rest."

We stand quietly for a few minutes sipping on our hot chocolate and watching the people milling about. When a few kids start throwing snowballs, I laugh. "That's what I missed out on as a kid. When I have children I want to live someplace with four seasons so they can experience the same thing."

"Kids, huh?"

"Maybe, someday. How about you?"

"I don't think it will happen."

"Yeah, you'd have to settle down with one woman."

Max turns to me and narrows his eyes. "That's not why. But feel free to keep making assumptions. I'm going to go back to the hotel."

As he walks away, he shouts over his shoulder, playing to the crowd, "Don't stay out here too late, babe. You'll freeze to death."

"I'll be in soon, babe," I say cheerfully. Two can play this game.

CHAPTER 4
ICE, ICE, BABY

When I walk into the bar at the ice hotel the next evening, my breathing becomes shallow and my heart rate starts to increase. Before you ask, it's not because Max manages to make one of those goofy hats with dog ear-flaps look sexy. No, the reason for my physical reaction is because this building is made entirely out of water.

Let's think about this for a moment, shall we? Buildings should be made out of sturdy materials, like brick, wood, or steel, not out of liquids. Liquids are, well, liquidy. Making a building out of something you can pour out of a glass is just nuts.

It's bad enough we're having drinks and dinner at a hotel made of ice, but I also have to spend the night here. What if it melts while I'm sleeping?

"Everyone, gather around," Lumi says, interrupting my thoughts about waking up in the middle of a large puddle. "I hope you all had fun today ice fishing."

I glance over at Max. He's grinning ear to ear, still thrilled about the fish he caught. I had wisely decided not to participate in the ice fishing—ice has a nasty habit of cracking, you know. Instead, I attended a workshop where we learned how to make himmeli, traditional Finnish Christmas ornaments made out of straw. Spending time apart from Max had been a good thing, especially how we had left things the previous night.

"Those of you who opted to stay overnight here, please come see me after dinner for an orientation session." Lumi chuckles. "Sleeping in an ice hotel is a little different from a regular hotel."

I take a deep breath and then exhale slowly, trying to calm my nerves. I definitely didn't *opt* to stay here. It's part of my assignment. I've had to do some crazy things in my time, but I gotta say, staying in an ice hotel tops the list.

Max walks over and hands me a shot glass. "What are you thinking about?"

"Global warming. I hope it doesn't happen tonight."

Max gives me a funny look. "You realize that's not how it works, right?"

"Doesn't staying here freak you out?" I ask.

"No, it'll be fun." He cocks his head to one side. "What's going on?"

"It's nothing," I say, not wanting to give Max an opportunity to make fun of me.

He motions at the glass in my hand.

"Okay, then. Drink up. Vodka is traditional."

I take a small sip. "Mmm . . . it tastes like candy canes."

He furrows his brow. "I thought you didn't like candy canes."

"Uh . . . about that." I take another sip. This stuff is delicious. There's no way I can go on pretending I'm not crazy about candy canes. I want to finish this drink. So I shrug and say nonchalantly, "I lied."

"Why?" When I don't respond, a smile creeps across Max's face. "I know why. This is because of that flight attendant who gave me the candy cane. You thought I was flirting with her. And in a moment of jealous rage, you made up some ridiculous story about not liking candy canes."

I finish my vodka, then say, "You've got quite an active imagination."

He smirks, then points at my empty glass. "Want another one?"

I'm torn. It was delicious, but one drink is plenty for me. Two might make things dangerous, especially where Max is concerned. He does look sexy in the hat, despite the goofy dog ear-flaps. Or is that because of the dog ear-flaps?

"No thanks, I'll pass," I say, meaning more than the vodka.

* * *

When we go into the dining room, I notice that the tables and benches are all made of ice. Personally, I think wood furniture wouldn't be amiss, but I suppose when you've got a theme, you go for it. Fortunately, the benches are covered with blankets, so I'm not freezing when I sit.

As the waiter places steaming bowls of soup in front of us, Lumi tells the group, "This is lohikeitto, a salmon chowder with a light cream broth."

Before I can try any, Max asks me to

hold off for a few moments while he takes pictures. A lot of our readers are real foodies and they love photos of traditional dishes from around the world.

After he finishes, Max sits across from me. As I dig in, he asks, "How is it?"

"Delicious," I say. "That is, if you like chunks of salmon, leeks, and potatoes."

"Who doesn't?" Max savors his soup, then asks, "There's a flavor in here I can't place."

"I heard Lumi say that it's allspice," I say. "It gives it quite a unique taste."

We talk about the different foods we've tried around the world while we eat. When our soup dishes are cleared, Max leans forward. "I've noticed that you never seem to take any notes."

I tap the side of my head. "I file it all away up here."

"How do you remember everything when it comes time to write your articles?" Max asks.

"Good memory, I guess," I say.

"I could never do that," Max says. "I have to write everything down at the end of each day or else I forget."

"Oh, my gosh, do you keep a diary?" I ask with a light mocking tone in my voice. "I used to have one when I was a girl. It was pink and had a little lock on it. What color is yours?"

Before I can tease Max some more, the waiter serves our main course— sautéed reindeer served with lingonberries, mashed potatoes, and pickled cucumbers.

"I know this is a traditional dish in Lapland," I say. "But I'm not so sure about eating reindeer."

"You've had venison, haven't you?" Max asks. "It's probably similar."

I sample the meat cautiously, then smile. "It's surprisingly good."

Max grins. "Told you so."

As he piles mashed potatoes on his fork, I say, "You're one of those guys who always has to be right, aren't you?

My ex was like that."

"Me? I'm rarely right about anything." He chews thoughtfully for a moment then says, "I was wrong about you."

I set down my fork and stare at him. "What's that supposed to mean?"

"Never mind," Max says.

"Don't you 'never mind' me," I say sharply. "I want to know what you meant by that."

"People are staring at us," Max says in an undertone.

"So?"

"We're supposed to be head over heels in love," he reminds me. "Why don't we change the subject and get back to pretending that we're a happy couple?"

"Fine. What do you want to talk about?"

"Why don't you tell me how you got into travel writing?"

"It's not all that interesting," I say. "When I studied journalism in college, I thought I would end up working for a newspaper. But things didn't work out that way. So instead of reporting on politics or world events, I write boring articles about what people do on vacation."

"They're not boring," Max says. "You're a great writer. When people read your articles they feel like they're right there with you experiencing what you're experiencing. That takes talent."

"Thanks, I guess."

"I'm being serious. I'm not right about much, but I am right about this—you're great at what you do."

"Talk about mixed messages," I say. "First you tell me that you were wrong about me, now you tell me you're right about me. Which is it?"

"I've always known you were a talented writer, but I was wrong about some other stuff." Before I can ask him to clarify, Max holds up his hand. "We can talk more about it in our room tonight."

I almost choke on the pickled cucumbers I'm eating when I realize what he just said. "*Our* room? We're sharing a room?"

Max gives me a mischievous grin. "Yeah, didn't I mention that before?"

* * *

As we wait for Lumi to show us to our room after dinner, I nudge Max. "Why don't we let someone else stay here? You know, an actual couple."

"There's two of us. That makes us a couple."

"Okay, technically we are a couple of . . . um . . . work colleagues, but we're not a couple in the romantic sense."

"Work colleagues, huh? Is that how you see us?"

"We're here for work. That makes us colleagues." I look at Max. "Why? What were you thinking we were? Friends?"

Max holds my gaze. "Not exactly."

"You think we're more than friends?" I splutter. "Let's get one thing straight, just because we're sharing a room doesn't mean anything is going to happen."

As Lumi approaches us, she asks, "Is everything okay?"

Max slings his arm around my shoulders. "Zoe is just worried about how cold it's going to get tonight."

Actually, my biggest worry is if we're going to get an unexpected heat wave and the ice hotel is going to melt. Well, that and the fact I'm going to be sharing a bed with Max.

"Oh, don't worry. You'll be snug as a rug in a bug," Lumi says. "Come, let me show you."

Max smiles. "I think you mean the reverse—a bug in a rug."

"Ah, yes. That makes more sense," she says. "I've studied English since I was a child, but I still make mistakes.

Do either of you speak other languages?"

"French and a little bit of Italian," I say.

"Spanish and Tagalog for me," Max says.

Lumi nods, then shows us our room. When we walk inside, she points out the reindeer hides on the bed. The bed, of course, is fashioned completely out of frozen water. "This will provide insulation from the ice. And these thermal sleeping bags will keep you toasty. There are also lots of blankets which you can pile on top of you if you need."

Max winks at me. "We can also cuddle and share our body heat to stay warm."

"I don't think that will be necessary," I say. "Those sleeping bags look plenty warm."

"These might help as well," Lumi says as she hands each of us a pair of woolen socks. "Compliments of the hotel."

"They're beautiful," I say, inspecting the intricate pattern.

"They're made locally," Lumi says. "Now, you remember the way back to the annex where you stored your belongings? Unlike the rest of the hotel, that building is heated. The bathrooms are located there, and you'll also have your breakfast there in the morning."

After checking to make sure we're all set, Lumi bustles off to get the rest of the group settled.

After she leaves, Max grabs one of the sleeping bags from the bed and places it on the floor.

"What are you doing?" I ask.

"Getting some shut eye. We have a big day tomorrow."

I furrow my brow. "You're sleeping on the floor? You realize it's made of ice, don't you?"

"So's the bed. It's basically one giant Popsicle."

"But it's covered in reindeer hides and

furs. Don't be an idiot. We can share the bed." I grab his sleeping bag and place it back on the bed.

"Nah, I can sleep on the floor. I don't want to tempt you with all this," he says, gesturing at himself.

"First, there's nothing tempting about you whatsoever."

"Not even the smell of my new candy cane cologne?"

"Candy cane cologne? There's no such thing."

"Sure is. I got a sample of it at the gift store." Max removes his scarf, then unzips his jacket. He leans down so that his neck is less than an inch from my mouth. "Can't you smell that?"

As I inhale sharply, I smell peppermint with faint undertones of something musky. It's intoxicating. Just a few drops of cologne and Max has turned into some sort of sexy candy cane. I feel myself start to tremble and I'm aching to press my lips against his neck.

Pull yourself together, Zoe, I admonish myself. Stepping back, I say in a bored tone, "Doesn't really smell like a candy cane to me. More like bubblegum. Anyway, where was I? Oh, yeah, second, even if there was anything tempting about you, it's freezing in here. What kind of hanky-panky do you think we'd get up to here? And third, I'm not that kind of girl."

"I'm not that kind of guy either."

"You're exactly that kind of guy. You're a flirt."

"I'm friendly," Max says. "There's a difference."

"Oh, please, you flirt with every woman you come across."

"Okay, fine, maybe I am a bit of a flirt," Max admits. "But it certainly doesn't mean I'm that 'kind of guy.'"

"Flirting is what's gotten you into this mess—having to pretend that we're a couple. Girls like Barbie think you like them."

"That's the problem. It's always the wrong girls who think I like them, never the right ones," Max mutters.

I give him a questioning look, but he just climbs into his sleeping bag, rolls over on his side and closes his eyes.

* * *

I can't sleep. I've been tossing and turning for what seems like hours. Thoughts of Max dressed up as a giant candy cane fill my mind. It's disturbing on so many levels.

I start to feel warm, as though I have a fever. How is it possible that I'm sweating in the middle of a room made of ice? I fling the blankets off me, then unzip my sleeping bag. Cool air rushes over my body, but I still feel like my skin is on fire. I sit up and inspect my surroundings. Is it my imagination or is water dripping from the corners of the room? Are those puddles forming on the floor?

I shake Max. "Wake up, the hotel is melting."

He opens his eyes and looks at me blearily. "Melting? We're in Finland in the dead of winter. It's freezing. How could the place be melting? Unless you're having a meltdown. That seems more like it."

I rub my eyes and look around again. Everything looks normal. What happened to the dripping water and the puddles? Did I just have one of those waking dreams? Considering Max played a starring role as a giant candy cane, it was more like a nightmare really.

Max sits up and puts his arm around me. "Hey, what's going on? You're shivering."

"Just a bad dream. Sorry I woke you."

"Tell me about it," he says gently. "It'll make it less real and then you'll be able to go back to sleep."

My eyes widen. There's no way I can tell him what I really dreamed about, so I make something up on the fly. "Remember the lead dog when we went sledding?"

"Into?"

"That's the one. I dreamed that I adopted him."

"That doesn't sound so scary."

"Ah, well it turns out he was really a werewolf."

"So, you're scared of werewolves and hedgehogs? Interesting."

I ignore the barb. "What were you dreaming about when I woke you? Do you remember?"

He says quietly, "You."

"Me?"

He nods.

"So a nightmare," I say, trying to lighten the mood.

"No, dreaming about you isn't scary. Now, my ex, that's a different story."

"I don't think I've heard about her."

"She's a photographer."

"Travel photography?"

"Um . . . not exactly."

"What does that mean?" I ask.

"She takes photos of shirtless guys."

"Seriously? That's a profession?"

"Apparently. You see them all the time on romance novels."

"Not the ones I read."

"You like romance books?"

"There's nothing wrong with that," I say defensively.

"I never said there was. My mom reads them. I've read some of them too." He smiles. "That's why I'm so great with the ladies. You can pick up a lot of tips in them."

"Like not wearing a shirt?" He laughs, then I tentatively ask, "Why did you guys break up?"

"Turns out she likes guys who don't wear shirts. I came back early from a trip and caught her with one of the models."

"Oh, that sucks. I'm sorry."

"Thanks. It happened a couple of years ago," he says. "It's not like we were planning on getting married or anything, so it's not really a big deal. We actually hadn't been together that long."

"Of course it's a big deal. Cheating is cheating no matter how long you've been together."

"Maybe that's why I'm such a big flirt now. I never used to be. I only paid attention to girls I was serious about, but now it's like I'm playing the field in a way. Not literally, though. It's not like I date a lot." Max presses his lips together, then looks at me. "So what about you? What's your story?"

"I don't have a story."

"Well, you have an ex, so you must have a story. Why did you guys break up? Is it because he always had to be right?"

"That's part of it. It's not like he's a bad guy or anything. He was just so serious and, well, boring."

"Then why were you with him?"

"I don't know. It was easy, I guess. Some mutual friends fixed us up on a blind date and that led to another date and another one and the next thing you know we were a couple." I sighed. "Then one day, I suggested that we go to the carnival. He refused. He told me that those types of things were for kids. When I got upset, he told me that when we had a family of our own, then we would go."

"A family? So you guys were engaged?"

"No, thankfully not. That's when I realized he was not the guy I wanted to spend the rest of my life with. It feels like a lucky escape."

"For what it's worth, I love carnivals," Max says. "Especially eating cotton candy on the Ferris wheel."

I grin. "That's my favorite too."

"I'm sure there are lots of guys lining

up to take you to the carnival," Max says.

I shake my head. "In my line of work it's hard to date. I'm always traveling from assignment to assignment. You know what it's like."

"Yeah, I do. I think that's part of why my ex cheated on me."

"No, she cheated on you because she's a bad person, not because you traveled."

"But that didn't help matters."

"I guess it takes a special kind of person who understands this lifestyle." Max locks his eyes with mine, then bends his head toward mine. I can smell his intoxicating candy cane cologne. I can sense his lips getting nearer to mine. I can . . .

"What did that person just yell?" I ask, pulling back. "Did they just say that the hotel is melting?"

CHAPTER 5
THE DANGER OF PROPANE SPACE HEATERS

Turns out the hotel was actually melting. One of the other guests worried she was going to freeze to death, so she smuggled in a propane space heater. Here's the problem with space heaters —they make ice melt. Apparently, this lady didn't quite grasp that concept.

Had my dream been some sort of premonition? Possibly. The hotel did melt, after all. I just hope that the part about being dressed up as a candy cane never comes true. That would be way too weird.

Although the manager assures us that the space heater only melted a small portion of the ice hotel, they've still decided that it would be safer to send us back to our regular hotel for the remainder of the night.

While we wait for the shuttle bus to pick us up, Max pulls out a soft leather-bound book from his backpack and opens it to a blank page.

"Is that your diary?" I ask.

Max uncaps a fountain pen and says firmly, "It's a journal, not a diary."

"Same thing. When I had a diary, I wrote down what happened each day. What do you write about in your diary?"

"Again, it's a journal," he says. "I make notations about my observations, incidents, and phenomena in it."

"That's basically a fancy way of saying you write down what happened each day. You know what else I used to record in my diary? What boys I had a crush on and if any of them tried to kiss me. Do you write stuff like that in your diary too?"

"For the last time, it's a journal—"

I hold my hand up. "Fine, we can call it a journal if you want."

"Thank you." Max shifts his body away from me and bends over his journal . . . er, diary.

"Are you writing about what happened tonight?" I ask, trying to peer over his shoulder.

He laughs and covers the page with his arm. "You mean about that woman and her space heater?"

"Well, that was interesting," I say. "But I was thinking more along the lines about how you almost kissed me."

Max twists his body and looks at me. "Me? You were the one who almost kissed me. Again."

"That's not how I remember it."

"Weren't you telling me what a good

memory you had earlier this evening?" He grins and taps the side of my head. "You don't have to take notes because you remember everything."

I inhale sharply as he runs his fingers from the side of my head down to my mouth. As he lightly traces my bottom lip, he whispers, "It's a shame we were interrupted and you couldn't kiss me like you wanted to."

"You mean you couldn't kiss me like *you* wanted to." I lean in closer, smelling his peppermint cologne, daring him to press his lips to mine.

"The bus is here," the manager calls out, startling both of us. Max's journal goes flying across the floor.

"I'll get it," I say. When I bend to pick it up, I notice several sheets of loose paper scattered nearby and gather them up.

"Please don't look at those," Max says.

"Too late," I say, stacking the pages

together. Each one is a sketch of different places in Santa's Village. "These are amazing. You're a very talented artist."

"No, I'm not." Max grabs the sketches from me, then shuffles through them. "There's one missing."

I look around and spot it under the bench we were sitting on. As I pick it up, my eyes widen. "Hey, this one's of me." I peer more closely at the sketch, recognizing the background. "Did you draw this when we were on the German riverboat cruise? This was right after we kissed, wasn't it? And you've been carrying it around this whole time? Why?"

Max shoves the paper back into his journal. "I don't know how that got stuck in here. I meant to throw it out."

Why don't I believe him?

* * *

The next day, I wake up and stretch my arms over my head and think about the previous night—the heart-to-heart we had about our exes, the almost-kiss (and for the record, he almost kissed me, not the other way around), and the fact that Max has been carrying a sketch of me around for months.

I have to admit, it's a really flattering sketch. I'm leaning over the railing of the riverboat, lost in thought, oblivious to the quaint German town on the shore. My hair is fluttering in the breeze, I'm holding a straw hat in one hand, and I'm wearing a polka-dot sundress.

The dress is how I know exactly when Max made the sketch. I had bought it in a boutique earlier that day and worn it to dinner that night. While we were walking on deck later that night, Max had joked about how the polka dots reminded him of M&M'S.

Then that infamous kiss happened. I grabbed Max's hand, and pulled him into an embrace. He looked surprised, but as soon as I pressed my lips against his, he made a noise that sounded like a cross between a growl and a moan. Then he ran his fingers through my hair, drawing me in closer and deepening the kiss.

This is just a pretend kiss, I kept telling myself. *It doesn't mean anything.*

Finally, I managed to pull myself away. Turning around, I saw my friend Isabelle give me a thumbs up sign. I nodded, then looked at Max. "Thanks. I think that fooled Erich."

"Erich? Who's Erich?" Max narrowed his eyes. "Wait a minute, does this have to do with Isabelle and that guy?"

"Yep, we were just doing her a favor." I toyed with the ribbon on my straw hat. "Thanks for playing along."

"So this didn't mean anything?" Max asked.

"Of course not," I said. "Remember, we can't stand each other. We'd be the last person either of us would want to kiss, right?"

Max pressed his lips together. "You're right. It didn't mean anything."

Then he turned and walked away, and I leaned over the railing, lost in thought about Max and that kiss that didn't mean anything.

My phone buzzes, interrupting my memories of that evening in Germany. When I pick it up, Max tells me that I'm late. I notice that this time his tone is light and joking, not like all the other times when he was so obviously irritated with my tardiness. "Better get a move on, babe. We're late for our appointment at Elf Central."

It almost feels like Max and I are a real couple, not just a pretend one. We connected last night, really connected. He's a nomad like me, constantly traveling for work, having no real roots. When I'm not on assignment, I stay with my sister and her family in Los Angeles.

Max crashes with a friend in New York City. Neither of us has a real home.

As I get dressed, I wonder what a home really is. Is it a physical building, whether a small bungalow, an apartment, or even a house made of ice? Or is a home something less tangible? A feeling you have when you've found someone to share your life with—they become your home.

Snap out of it, I tell myself as I pull on my favorite sweater—the pink one with candy canes on it. *You're getting entirely too mushy. Whatever happened between you and Max last night was a fluke. Just wait and see. Things will be back to normal in no time with the two of you not being able to stand each other.*

* * *

When I walk into the hotel lobby, Max is chatting with the desk clerk. He must be telling the most hilarious jokes because she can't stop laughing. When Max smiles at the woman, I feel myself stiffen. Yep, the old Max is back. The one who can't help but flirt with every woman in his path.

"You ready?" I say brusquely to Max. "Or are the two of you busy?"

"I was the one waiting for you, remember?" he says coolly.

"Max was just telling me the hedgehog story," the young woman says in between giggles. "I can't believe you mistook a hedgehog for a rattlesnake. And then you jumped up onto a chair and screamed, 'Killer Snake.' It's a good thing Max caught the hedgehog when it went flying. It could have been hurt."

"It was an easy mistake. Rattlesnakes are all over the place in Arizona," I snap. "If Max hadn't put that creature on my shoulder without warning me first, none of that would have happened."

"I did tell you, but you were too busy

chatting on the phone with your boyfriend—"

I hold up my hand. "Ex-boyfriend. And that's still no excuse for what you did."

"I thought it would make a cute picture. The whole group was taking turns getting their picture taken with it. Besides, everyone loves hedgehogs."

I put my hands on my hips. "Not everyone."

"Well, I know that now," Max says stiffly.

"Let's not talk about it anymore, okay? We're late."

"No, we're not. Once I realized you were still sleeping when I called you, I phoned the Chief Elf and asked him if we could push back our appointment by an hour." Max looks at his watch. "We have twenty minutes to get there. Plenty of time."

"You didn't have any right to reschedule it. This is my interview. You're just tagging along to take pictures."

The desk clerk looks back and forth at us warily, then smiles brightly at me. "Max told me you're going to do an article on the elves who work at Santa's Village. That sounds fascinating."

Actually, it does sound fascinating—a behind-the-scenes peek at how Santa's Village operates—but there's no way I'm going to agree with Miss "Max is My Hero for Catching that Hedgehog," especially not after the way she keeps batting her eyelashes at him.

"It's just part of the job," I say, then stride toward the door.

Max and I walk to Elf Central in silence. I glance at him, wondering what he's thinking about. Probably the desk clerk.

Shaking my head, I focus on the interview and the questions I'm going to ask. From my research, I know that because Santa's Village gets visitors from around the world, the elves are recruited based in part on their ability to speak multiple languages. I suppose one of the other key factors in hiring them is their willingness to wear fake pointy elf ears. I'm eager to learn more about the hiring process and what it takes to get a job here.

When Max and I arrive at Elf Central, I pause to admire the building. It looks like an over-sized gingerbread house. If I didn't know better, I'd swear that the colorful decorations on the outside were made of real candy.

As soon as I enter the building, I start to break out in a sweat. This feels exactly like last night when I had that nightmare about the ice hotel melting. I remove my hat and mittens, and unzip my coat. "Why is it so hot in here?" I mutter.

An elf wearing a red short-sleeved t-shirt that shows off his muscular chest greets us. Suspenders and plaid pants complete the look. Wow, who knew elves could be so sexy. Then I look down, expecting to see felt boots. Instead I see a pair of incredibly hairy feet. You can't even see this guy's toenails through all that hair. Wow, I know it's roasting in here, but going barefoot isn't exactly a good look for you, buddy.

After the Chief Elf introduces himself —his name is Eldon—he apologizes. "Sorry, we're having a problem with the central heating."

A female elf named Edwina joins us. She's sporting a similar look—red t-shirt, a plaid skirt, and hairy bare feet. Max seems oblivious to her foot situation, probably because her t-shirt is at least one size too small for her.

They lead us over to a large wooden trestle table. Eldon pours us coffee while Edwina sets down a platter of joulutorttu—star-shaped Christmas cookies made out of flaky pastry and filled with prune jam.

After sampling some of the cookies, Max takes pictures while I conduct the interview.

"Those ears look so real," I say. "Do they take a long time to put on?"

"But they are real." Eldon laughs and tugs at the top of one of his pointy ears.

I feel my face redden. I'm inadvertently mocking Eldon's misshapen ears. He can't help it if he was born with them. "I'm so sorry."

He furrows a brow. "Why are you sorry? All elves have ears like these."

"Of course, it's what visitors expect elves to look like. I suppose you're lucky that you don't have to wear fake ones." As the words come out of my mouth, I realize that I'm just making things worse. I try to change the subject, but hearing Max chuckle behind me makes me even more flustered.

I spin around and give him a warning look. He just grins and snaps a picture of me.

"Are you one of those people who doesn't believe in Santa Claus and elves?" Edwina asks. "We get a few of them up here."

"Oh, I see what's going on," I say. "You guys are pulling my leg. The ears aren't real."

Eldon smiles. "The ears are real and we're really elves."

"I suppose Santa is real too," I say.

"Yes," Edwina says.

Eldon leans across the table and says conspiratorially, "Off the record, Santa is a busy man at this time of year, so he does have some helpers who stand in for him."

I might have rolled my eyes a little bit because Max says, "Come on, Zoe, get into the Christmas spirit. How can anyone visit Santa's Village and not believe in the man himself?"

"Shouldn't you be taking pictures?" I say.

Max shrugs and wanders around the

large room, taking photos of the Christmas decorations. Edwina happily poses for him in front of the fire, and the two of them engage in flirtatious banter. Apparently, hairy toes don't seem to be a turn-off for Max.

Eldon and I continue the interview, talking about the most popular toys these days. While I sip on my coffee, I ask what he does during the summer.

"What do you mean? Christmas is a year-round thing. There's always lots to do."

"You must get vacation. Where do you go?"

"Oh, vacation. Sure, we get time off. Last year, I went to the Bahamas. This year I'm not sure where I want to go. What would you recommend?"

"Definitely not Mongolia," I say before making a few suggestions. "Ravenna in Italy is nice and the riverboat cruises in Germany are amazing."

Max wanders over. I notice that he's

wearing one of those red and green felt elf hats. For some reason, it looks strange on someone with normal ears. He models it for me. "This was a gift from Edwina."

"Why don't you get one for Zoe, as well?" Eldon says to Edwina.

"No, that's okay," I say, pointing at my mint green hat. "My grandma knitted this for me. She knits all my hats. They're the only ones I wear."

"That's sweet," Edwina says. "My grandmother knits socks."

I glance down at her feet, thinking a pair of socks wouldn't be a bad idea.

After a few more minutes discussing knitting patterns, Max and I take our leave. As we walk outside he asks, "Did you get what you need from the interview?"

"Kind of. I'm not really sure how I'm going to write it up. People who believe they're really elves? I'm going to have to talk with Nicole about it."

"So you really don't believe that they're elves?"

"Of course not," I say. "Don't tell me you do."

Max gives me a considered look. "You'd be surprised what I believe in."

"Like what?"

"Well, when I was a kid, my dad used to read me bedtime stories. One of them was about how Santa's elves could fix anything using only magic. One day, when my toy train broke, I was absolutely devastated. My dad told me he was going to take it to the elves to fix. The next week, it was back, good as new."

"Did you ever stop to think that it was new?" I say. "Your dad probably went out and bought a new one."

"Nope, I know for sure that it was the elves who did it." He smiles at me. "Who knows, maybe one day you'll need elven magic to fix something."

CHAPTER 6
REINDEER DROOL

I had another restless night, waking up several times mid-nightmare in a cold sweat with my heart pounding in my ears. The details of my bad dreams are fuzzy, but I do know that they all had one thing in common—Max surrounded by gorgeous women vying for his attention. He's in his element, flirting with all of them, while I stand off in the background unnoticed.

I grab one of the pillows and hug it to my chest. It's bad enough that I have to deal with Max during the day. Why does he have to ruin my sleep by haunting my dreams?

I need to get to the bottom of these nightmares. There's gotta be some sort of symbolism hidden in them. If I can figure out what it is, maybe I'll be able to get a good night's sleep. Knowing that my sister is into dream analysis, I give her a call. After filling her in on the events of the previous day—the interview at Elf Central, followed by a snowmobile excursion in the evening to see the Northern Lights—I tell her about my nightmares.

"Let me see if I've got this straight," my sister says. "You dreamed that Max was flirting with other women and ignoring you."

"That's the basic gist," I say. "What does it mean? You have one of those dream dictionaries, don't you?"

"Yeah, I don't need a dictionary to figure this one out," she says dryly. "The meaning is obvious."

I sit up in bed, eager to hear what her interpretation is. "Do the other girls represent different career paths? Should I give up travel writing and move back to California and learn how to decorate cakes? Or maybe teach Pilates?"

My sister laughs. "No, it's a lot simpler than that. You're in love with Max and you're afraid he doesn't feel the same way."

"In love with Max?" I splutter. "Absolutely not. You're crazy."

"Am I?" she says. "You talk about him all the time."

"That's only because we work together," I say. "And if I do talk about him, it's to complain. I'm totally indifferent to him."

"Uh-huh. Maybe you should look up the meaning of 'indifferent' in the dictionary because that's not what it means."

"Okay, maybe I'm not completely indifferent, but that's because he's a complete jerk. Remember that whole hedgehog incident?"

"You know, that story is kind of funny. But, I know you. You hate to look foolish, especially by a guy you like." She laughs, then says in a more serious tone, "Let me offer you a bit of big sisterly advice. You tried to play it safe with Carl. He was the type of guy who would have offered you security. A professional with a good job who could have taken care of you and provided for a family."

"Carl was a nice guy," I say.

"I'm not saying he wasn't. But, let's face it, he was boring. The life you would have led with him would have been boring. And you're anything but boring, Zoe. You're free-spirited. You love to travel and go on adventures. You need someone who has the same approach to life. Someone like Max."

I chew on my bottom lip. "He is adventurous, I'll give you that, but he's definitely not the kind of guy I can see myself with long-term."

"Listen, we've all got baggage that leads to the stories we tell ourselves. Maybe yours is baggage about how our dad left when we were little kids because of another woman. Maybe it's because mom was constantly trying to make ends meet while raising us on her own, and we ended up having to move around a lot. But just because that's how we grew up doesn't mean you have to settle for a traditional kind of guy and a traditional kind of life."

"But you did," I say. "You got married and now you're a stay-at-home mom in the suburbs."

"The key word here is *settle*," she says. "I didn't settle. I chose the perfect life and the perfect guy for me. But just because it's the right path for me, doesn't mean it's the right path for you. For you, it'd be *settling*."

"Do you really think so?" I say faintly.

"Sorry, Zoe, I have to go. The baby's crying." My sister pauses for a moment, then adds, "Just think about what I said, okay? My gut is telling me that Max is the perfect guy for you—someone who leads an adventurous, nomadic life just like you do. Maybe it's time you admitted that to yourself?"

* * *

I think about what my sister said during the bus ride to the reindeer farm. Maybe she's right. Not about Max, of course. She's dead wrong about him. I don't want a guy who's constantly flirting with other women. Sure, he says that it doesn't mean anything, but what if one day a flirtation led to something more serious? What if he ends up running out on me like my dad ran out on my mom?

As boring as Carl was, I knew that he never would have flirted with anyone else, let alone cheated on me. My sis may have been right that I should look for an adventurous guy who loves to travel, but Max definitely isn't that guy.

"Hey, Max, want to go out for a drink tonight?" Barbie leans across the aisle and puts her hand on his knee.

Max shakes his head. "Sorry, Zoe and I have plans."

Rather than stiffen when Max puts his arm around my shoulder, I snuggle into him, giving Barbie a look that says, "He's all mine." Pretend mine, that is. He'll never be the real mine. I'll never let that happen.

When we get to the reindeer farm, Lumi says, "Before we get off the bus, let me tell you a few things about today's activity. This farm is owned by a Sámi couple. The Sámi are the indigenous inhabitants of Sápmi, what you might know as Lapland. They're traditionally a semi-nomadic people known for reindeer herding. Normally, their reindeer roam free, but they round them up twice a year."

"If everyone lets their reindeer run free, how do they know which ones are theirs?" someone asks from the rear of the bus.

"They put notches on their ears," Lumi explains. "Kind of like branding cattle."

I turn and see Christopher bouncing in his seat. "How many reindeer do they have?" he asks.

"Ah, that's a very good question," Lumi says. "It's actually rude to ask the Sámi how many reindeer they own. It would be like asking someone how much money they make."

Lumi consults her clipboard, then says, "We're going to go on a sleigh ride to a kota; that's a traditional hut. We'll have grilled sausages there before we return back here."

"Can we pet the reindeer?" one of the other kids asks.

"Even better." Lumi smiles. "You can feed them."

When Max and I get off the bus, Lumi pulls us aside. "It took a lot of convincing to get permission for the two of you to drive one of the sleighs, but I managed to do it. The sleighs are all tied together, so you don't have to worry about getting off course and crashing again."

"You mean they heard about what happened at the dog park?" I ask.

"Yes, it's all anyone can talk about in the village."

Max and I both look sheepish as we're led to our assigned sleigh. After we're seated and reindeer hides are piled on top of us to keep out the chill, I lean into Max.

He pulls away and folds his arms across his chest. "We're at the rear. No one can see us back here. We don't need to pretend right now."

"Fine with me," I say, shifting over to the other side of the seat.

The sleigh ride should have been fun. Being pulled by reindeer through a snowy meadow is a dream for kids of all ages. Instead, all I can think about is the tension in the air between Max and me. Things were fine between us yesterday. Sure, we were pretending to be a couple, but it wasn't awkward like this is.

When we pull up in front of the kota, Lumi jokes, "Congratulations, you didn't crash."

Max slings his arm around me and gives me an adoring look. "Thank goodness. I'd be beside myself if anything happened to the love of my life."

Give the man an Academy Award. Lumi looks totally convinced by his performance.

"Oh, that's my phone," I say, pulling it out of my pocket. "It's Nicole. I wonder what she wants."

"You better take that, babe," Max says. "I'll meet you inside."

"Everything okay?" I ask Nicole.

"Um, well not exactly," she says. "It's

about Max."

"Is something wrong? He's not his usual self today."

Nicole takes a deep breath. "I suppose I better just come out and say it. Max emailed me his resignation letter last night."

My jaw drops. "He did what? Why?"

"He said he can't work with you anymore. He said that it wouldn't be fair of him to put me in the position of choosing between the two of you, so he did the gentlemanly thing and resigned." Nicole's voice softens. "Honey, what happened between the two of you?"

I feel a knot forming in my stomach. Reluctant to tell her about the whole fake relationship, I eventually say, "I don't know."

"Well, just so you know, I told him I couldn't accept his resignation," Nicole says. "I asked him to think about it for a few days and that we'd talk after the holidays. You guys have two days left on your trip. Maybe you can convince him to change his mind during that time."

"I doubt it, but I'll do my best," I say, knowing that one way or another I'll probably never see Max again after this trip.

Some Christmas this turned out to be.

* * *

When I join the others in the kota, Max waves me over. "Saved you a spot, babe."

My confusion from Nicole's phone call has morphed into anger. How dare Max make me pretend to me his girlfriend just so that he doesn't get into trouble with the company because of Barbie? A company that he's resigning from? If he wants to continue this fake relationship for the next couple of days, I'm going to make sure that I play it for all it's worth.

"Thanks, babe," I say, laying my head

on his shoulder. "It was agony being separated for so long."

"Agony?" he whispers. "Don't you think you're overdoing it?"

"They're serving lunch," I say sweetly. "You wait right here, babe. I'll get you a plate."

"The two of you are such a cute couple," Christopher's mom says to me as we wait in line. "How long have you been together?"

"Honestly, it feels like forever," I say evasively.

"That's the way it is with my husband and I," she says. "It's hard not spending Christmas with him, but when you're married to someone who works offshore you don't get to spend every holiday together."

"That must be hard on Christopher," I say.

"It is. That's why I brought him to Santa's Village. I thought it would be a good distraction from not having his dad around." She glances over to where Max is sitting. "The two of you are lucky to be spending Christmas together."

"You have no idea," I say before blowing Max a kiss.

* * *

"What was that about?" Max asks when we leave the kota to go feed the reindeer.

"What do you mean?" I ask, batting my eyelashes and rubbing his bicep.

He yanks his arm away. "Why are you being so lovey-dovey?"

"You wanted everyone to be convinced that I'm your girlfriend. I'm convincing them."

He rolls his eyes. "I think you might be overdoing it. I'll meet you at the barn."

As he walks away I call out, "Babe, I'm sorry. I didn't mean to make you mad at me. Come back here and we can kiss and make up."

Max spins around, a fake smile plastered on his face, and rushes back to me. "No, I'm sorry, babe. It was my fault," he says loudly for everyone's benefit. Then he whispers in my ear, "What did you drink at lunch? Did you put a shot of vodka in your juice?"

"Just straight-up juice," I say.

He looks at me dubiously. "Well, I think you can tone it down. Barbie got the message. She hasn't tried hitting on me since I told her we were together."

"Seriously? Are you blind? She's been hitting on you constantly. She doesn't care if you have a girlfriend. She wants you. Period."

"We can talk about this later," Max says.

Lumi hands us some carrots. "Ready to feed the reindeer?"

While I walk around the barn, deciding which reindeer to give my carrots to, Max perches on a bale of hay, pulls out his journal, and starts sketching.

"I thought that was a secret," I say.

He shrugs. "You already know about it. And everyone else is too busy feeding the reindeer to notice."

"Why don't you make drawings from your photos later?"

"It's not the same thing. When you're drawing something from real life, it's magical." Max gives an embarrassed laugh. "I don't know how to explain it."

I reassure him. "You're doing fine."

"It's not something you can explain. You have to experience it for yourself." Max flips through his journal to a blank sheet of paper and hands me a pencil. Pointing at the reindeer in front of us, "Here, why don't you try it?"

"Me? I can't draw."

"Anyone can draw. We all learn to do it as kids. Don't tell me you didn't have crayons growing up."

"Yeah, but that doesn't make me an artist."

"Nonsense. You're an artist with

words. This is just a different way of expressing yourself. You can learn how to do it." Max walks behind me and puts his arms on my shoulders. "Take a long look at the reindeer. Now, close your eyes. Take a deep breath, picture the reindeer in your mind, and draw."

"With my eyes closed?"

"Yes, just let go and trust yourself."

As I trace the pencil on the paper, I can feel the heat of Max's body against my back, which is odd because we're both wearing down jackets and snow pants.

"Are you picturing the reindeer in your head?" Max asks.

No, I'm picturing you in my mind. You without a jacket, without a scarf, without a hat, without a shirt . . . *Stop it, Zoe. Focus on the antlered creature in front of you.*

Oblivious to the fantasy playing out in my head, Max rubs my shoulders, encouraging me to keep sketching. After a few minutes he removes his hands. "Okay, take a look."

I stare at the piece of paper in my hand. "It's just a bunch of scribbles."

"That's not what I see," Max says, coming round to sit next to me. "I see the essence of a reindeer."

More like the essence of a man without a shirt on, I think to myself.

Max leans closer to me, and for a moment I think he's going to kiss me. Then he pulls away abruptly. "I still have some carrots. I should go find a reindeer to give them to."

As I watch Max walk over to where Christopher and his mom are standing, I take a deep breath and wonder what just happened. Noticing that Max left his journal lying on the hay bale, I pick it up and wander over to compare my drawing to the reindeer in front of me.

I lean against the railing of the stall and hold the paper up. "Do you think that looks like you?"

Before the reindeer can respond, I'm distracted by Christopher and the other kids chanting, "We want Rudolph!"

When I turn back around, I gasp. The reindeer has Max's journal in his mouth. "What are you doing? That's not yours!" I try to yank it away, but the reindeer clamps down even harder. After a prolonged session of tug-of-war, I finally emerge victorious with a slimy journal in my hand.

I gulp when I see Max striding toward me.

"What did you do?" he asks, his eyes steely.

"Nothing," I say, trying to wipe the reindeer drool off with my scarf.

He snatches it from my hands. "You're supposed to feed reindeer carrots, not . . ." His voice trails off as he inspects his journal. "Almost half the pages have teeth marks on them and the other half are covered in saliva."

"I'm sorry," I say. "It was an accident."

"Way to go, babe," Max says before storming off.

CHAPTER 7
BABE OVERLOAD

I didn't dream last night. That's because I didn't sleep. I was up all night thinking about that jerk, Max. That man makes me so angry. Actually, I'm angry at myself. It's not Max's fault that he's a jerk. That's what he is. I've known that all along, but stupidly I tried to convince myself that he was something other than what he is.

I stare at my face in the mirror, trying to cover the dark circles under my eyes with concealer. It doesn't work. Well, who cares? I'm here to write a story about Santa's Village, not impress some stupid guy.

After getting dressed, I look out the window. It's still dark out, but I can make out fluffy snowflakes falling onto the fir trees. Growing up, my mom would take us to the beach on Christmas Eve, and we'd eat fried chicken while watching the surfers. Spending Christmas Eve in Finland certainly is different—snow, reindeer, and elves.

I glance at the clock and grin. If I hurry, I'll actually make it to breakfast on time. Quickly pulling my hair back into a loose bun, I head to the dining room with two minutes to spare. Take that, Max.

"You look gorgeous, babe," Max says when I take my seat next to him.

"Thanks," I say. "You look great too, babe."

I rub my temples. I am so tired of calling Max 'babe.'

Max gives me a concerned look. "Do you have a headache, babe?"

"Nope, I'm fine . . . babe." I look around the cozy dining room, then point at the straw ornament hanging over the table. "That's a himmeli. That's what I learned how to make when you were ice-fishing."

"Is it the Finnish equivalent of mistletoe?" Max asks.

Lumi hears us from across the table. "Oh, you young lovebirds, always looking for an excuse to kiss, aren't you?"

Max gives me a knowing look, but before he can take the charade too far, we're served breakfast.

"Finns traditionally eat rice porridge at Christmas time," Lumi explains. "We hide an almond in it and whoever gets it in their bowl will have good fortune."

Christopher looks at his bowl and scowls. "Can't I have regular cereal instead?"

His mom smiles. "Try some. Maybe you'll find the almond."

"Yum," Christopher says after taking a hesitant bite.

I have to agree, it is yum, probably because of all the butter, sugar, and cinnamon swirled in the bowl.

"I found it," Max cried out, doing a fist pump in the air. He holds up the almond and shows everyone.

"Congratulations, you'll have good fortune."

Max pops the almond in his mouth and looks at me. "How could my fortune be any better? I already have the best girl in the world."

Seriously? And he thought I was over-the-top pretending to be his fake girlfriend yesterday? This performance of his is gag-worthy. I put my napkin on the table and push back my chair. "You know what, babe, I do have a headache after all. I think I'm going to go lie down."

I can't believe it's come down to this—

faking a headache so that I don't have to fake being in love.

* * *

I avoid Max for the rest of the day, refusing to answer the phone when he calls and putting the pillow over my head to drown out the noise of him knocking on my door. When it's time for dinner, I text Max, telling him that I still have a headache, then order room service.

Just as I'm about to dig into my dessert—a cake made with wheat and almond flour, and flavored with ginger and cardamom—my phone rings. When I see that it's Nicole calling, guilt washes over me. Staying in my room all day is the height of unprofessionalism. How am I supposed to write an article about Christmas in Santa's Village when I've missed out on the Christmas Eve activities?

"I'm sorry," I say to Nicole. "I have no excuse for my behavior."

"What are you talking about?" she says.

"Isn't that why you called?"

"No, I called because I was worried about you. Max said that you've been sick all day. Are you okay? Do you need anything?"

I push back my dessert plate and slump in my chair. How can I enjoy cake when I'm nothing but a big fat liar? "I'm not sick," I say. "Just sick of Max."

"Sick of Max? But how? When I talked to him, he said that things were going well between you."

"Well?" I scoff. "Have I passed the fake girlfriend test?"

"Zoe, what's going on?" Nicole says slowly.

I tell her everything—how Max wanted us to pretend that we were a couple, the almost kiss in the ice hotel, the mixed messages Max kept sending me, and how much I hate calling someone "babe."

"Okay, let me see if I can get this straight," Nicole says. "Max told you I would fire him if someone else complained about him flirting?"

"Uh-huh, because of what happened in Sri Lanka."

Nicole laughs. "Wow, I have to give him points. Making up that whole story sure was one creative way of hooking up with you."

"Hang on a minute." I take a huge bite of the cake, hoping it will smother the anger bubbling up inside me. It does. Cake to the rescue again. Feeling a bit calmer, I say, "Basically, Max lied. This was all some sort of joke on his part like the thing with the hedgehog. He thought it would be funny to watch me pretend to be his girlfriend."

"Zoe, what am I going to do with you?" Nicole asks. "How can you not see what's right in front of your face? Max wants you to be his girlfriend for real, he just doesn't know how to go about it."

"Do you really think so?" When I realize that my voice just cracked, I shovel down some more cake.

"Yes, and you want to know what else I think? I think you want to be his girlfriend for real too. Think about it, okay?" Nicole says. "And, try to have a Merry Christmas."

After wishing Nicole a Merry Christmas, I stare at my empty plate for what seems like hours. Is it possible that my sister and Nicole are right? Do Max and I belong together?

I look at the clock and sigh. I have an idea, but it's too late to put it into action. But tomorrow morning, first thing, I'm heading to Elf Central. Maybe they can help me fix things.

CHAPTER 8
THE CASE OF THE
MISSING ELVES

Do you know how hard it is to track down an elf in Santa's Village on Christmas Day? I know, it surprised me too. I had always thought that once they loaded up the sleigh with presents and waved Santa and his reindeer goodbye, they were off the clock. It was time for those pointy-eared workers to kick back with a glass of glögi or eggnog in front of the fire at Elf Central.

Apparently not. Elf Central is deserted.

The only evidence that the elves have been here recently are the embers in the fireplace and a red and green cap lying on one of the overstuffed armchairs.

I wrap my arms around myself, wishing I hadn't forgotten my hat back at the hotel. The problem the elves had with their central heating seems to have gone in the opposite direction—instead of being boiling inside Elf Central, it's now freezing. Winter in Finland is brutal. I hope my next assignment is someplace warm, like India or the Australian outback.

I take a deep breath, and attempt to focus. If I'm going to pull off my surprise for Max, I need to find an elf. Maybe they're at Santa's Lodge?

Bracing myself to go back out in the snow in search of Santa's helpers, I grab the forgotten elf cap from the armchair. No, I'm not stealing it. Just borrowing it. The elves seem like understanding people. Besides, Eldon told me that they actually don't like wearing their caps. Unlike humans who are susceptible to frostbite, elfin folk are adapted for the cold, and their heads sweat profusely under their caps. That's why they have those pointy ears. They help radiate the heat away from their bodies.

But Santa is all about appearances, so he insists that the elves wear the red and green caps. One of the elves probably rebelled and "forgot" his cap back here at Elf Central. He or she will be cool with me wearing it. At least, I hope so. I don't want them to rat me out and put me on Santa's naughty list.

As I go to place the cap on my head, a card flutters onto the floor. I pick it up and smile at the illustration of the dancing elves on the front. They're barefoot, of course. When I open the card, I'm surprised to see that it's for me.

Dear Zoe – We hope you enjoy this cap. Merry Christmas from Eldon and Edwina.

I put my hand to my mouth. How did they know I was going to need a hat? How did they know I would come to Elf Central today?

No time to think about this now. I have to track down one of these elves. It's the only way I can make things right with Max. Pushing the door to Elf Central open, I step outside. Despite the frigid wind blowing, I feel warm and toasty as I run toward Santa's Lodge, and I'm pretty sure that's all due to the cap.

* * *

When I get to Santa's Lodge, I peer through the windows into the gift shop. The place is deserted too. Where is everyone? Although, I suppose it is Christmas Day. If you haven't bought your presents by now, you're out of luck.

Wondering if there are any elves in the back somewhere, I cautiously try the door. Finding it unlocked, I poke my head inside. "Yoo-hoo, is anyone here?" When no one replies, I push the door open and enter the building. Calling out again, I walk toward the back of the store. Not one single elf in sight, not in the stockroom, the break room, or the workshop where Santa Claus receives visitors.

I return to the gift shop, hoping I'll find what I need there. After wandering through all the aisles, I reluctantly give up. "There goes my plan," I mutter.

"What plan was that?" a voice behind me says.

I turn and see Max leaning against one of the counters. "How long have you been standing there?"

"Long enough to see you scurrying around like a madwoman looking for something."

"I'm surprised they leave this place

unlocked," I say, looking around at all the candy, souvenirs, and other trinkets on display.

"I'm not. This is Santa's Village. No one is going to steal from Santa Claus. That man always knows if someone is being naughty. You have to admit, it's a pretty effective security system." Max folds his arms across his chest. "Now, tell me what this plan of yours was."

"I wanted to fix your journal," I say. "It was going to be my Christmas present to you."

"There's no way you can fix it," Max says. "Those pages that the reindeer ate are gone forever."

"I know that, but I thought that one of the elves could fix it. I've been looking everywhere for them, but they're nowhere to be found."

"How could an elf fix it unless . . ." Max smiles at me. "Oh, I see what's happened. You believe in elfin magic now."

I look down at the ground. "Maybe. But it doesn't matter. There aren't any elves around."

Max rubs his jaw. "Okay, so you couldn't find an elf. But you were looking for something."

"I was looking for a replacement journal. I know it wouldn't be the same, but I thought it might help a little bit. But they don't have any."

"Hah, you called it a journal."

I put my hands on my hips. "I meant to say diary."

Max pushes himself off the counter and walks toward me. As he draws closer, I think about what my sister said to me. Is this man the perfect guy for me? Is it time I admitted that to myself and to him? I have taken a lot of risks in my life—like riding a yak across the Mongolian desert and bungee jumping off a cliff in Tahiti—but telling Max how I really feel? Well, that's possibly the riskiest thing I can do.

"I hate it when you flirt with other girls," I blurt out.

Max locks his eyes with mine. After a beat, he says, "Haven't you ever noticed that the only girl I don't flirt with is you?"

I furrow my brow, then fling my hands in the air. "That's my point. I have feelings for you and knowing that you don't feel the same way—"

Max puts a finger on my lips. "I have feelings for you too, Zoe. Serious feelings. Feelings that freak me out. Why do you think I don't flirt with you? Because I've been scared that something might happen between us."

I take a step back. "And you don't want anything to happen, right? You don't want a serious relationship, marriage, kids, anything like that?"

"Oh, I want kids one day," Max says. "I want them a lot. But I don't think it's going to happen."

I cock my head to one side. "Why?"

"Because of my career. I travel all the

SMITTEN WITH CANDY CANES 131

time. What woman is going to want to raise kids with me given my lifestyle?"

"Maybe a woman who also likes to travel all the time. A woman like me." I hold my hands up. "Listen, I'm not saying we're going to get married and have kids. I'm just saying that there are people out there who make a nomadic lifestyle work for their families."

Max contemplates this for a moment. "Nicole said the same thing to me."

"Yeah, speaking of Nicole, she told me you made up that whole story about that girl's boyfriend from Sri Lanka calling to complain about you. You were never in any danger of getting fired."

A sheepish grin creeps across Max's face. "So, she ratted me out."

I pace back and forth, then jab Max's chest. "So why did you want me to pretend to be your girlfriend?"

"Isn't it obvious? That's the only way I could get close to you. If I had asked you to go on a date, what would you have said?"

"No."

"Exactly."

We stare at each other for a moment, neither of us sure what to say next.

Max breaks the ice. "Cute hat."

"Thanks, it was a gift from the elves."

Max takes my hand in his. "What do you say? Should we try being a real couple and see where things go?"

"No more pretending?" I ask, my heart pounding in my chest.

He nods. "Out of curiosity, if we had gone through this entire trip pretending to be a couple, what was I going to owe you?"

"Oh, on our next trip together, I was going to make you wear a different costume each day." I smile. "I know how much you hate dressing up."

"Yeah, someday I'll have to tell you about what my brother did to me at Halloween one year. It's scarred me for life. I'll never wear a costume again."

"Never?"

"Never. You couldn't even pay me to dress up as Santa Claus. Speaking of . . ." Max smiles as he leads me into Santa's workshop. Just like in the gift shop, the lights are dim, and the only sound is that of Christmas carols playing softly in the background.

Max sits in Santa's green velvet chair, then pulls me onto his lap. "Have you been naughty or nice this year, Zoe?"

"Nice, of course." I run my fingers along his jawline, down to the cleft in his chin. "You, on the other hand, have been naughty."

"How so?"

"Flirting with all those girls."

"You're the only girl I want to flirt with." Max cups his hand behind my neck and pulls my face closer to his. "To think I fell in love with you that day on the riverboat in Germany."

I slide his shirt collar to one side, then shift my head so that my lips are nearly touching his neck. Breathing in his peppermint fragrance, I say, "You love me?"

"I do," Max says simply. Then he shifts ever so slightly, and my mouth presses against his skin. I trail kisses up his neck and gently nip his earlobe.

"You're driving me crazy," Max says, his voice low and husky. He takes control, brushing his lips against mine, softly at first, then more insistently. Now I'm being driven crazy.

Remembering where we are—in the middle of Santa's workshop, sitting on Santa's chair—I pull back. After looking around the room to make sure we're still alone, I slip off Max's lap. "That was the perfect first kiss."

Max chuckles. "It's actually our second kiss. Remember Germany?"

"Vaguely," I say with a teasing tone in my voice. "But, first, second, who's counting?"

"Oh, I'm counting." Max stands, then

pulls his battered journal out of his jacket pocket. He flips through the pages. When he reaches the one he's looking for, he says, "Good, this one is still intact." Turning to me, he asks, "Got something to write with?"

I reach into my purse and pull out a pen. He starts to grab it, but I yank it back. "I want to see what's on that page first."

A mischievous smile spreads across Max's face, then he hands the journal to me. My jaw drops when I read what he's written on the top of the page—"Kisses with Zoe." There's only one entry—the date and place that we first kissed in Germany. Underneath is a sketch of a trademark apple strudel that they served on the riverboat cruise.

I grin. "See, I told you this was a diary. You keep a record of the girls you kiss in here."

"Girl, singular, you mean. You're the only girl I've written about in here." Max shakes his head. "And it's a journal, not a diary. Can I have the pen now?"

After I hand it to him, he walks over to a counter, shielding the journal from view. When I try to see what he's writing, he gently pushes me aside. "Patience, Zoe."

After a few minutes, he waves me over and shows me his latest entry—today's date, followed by "Kiss Number Two, Santa's Village, Finland." Underneath is a sketch of a candy cane.

I look up at him and he takes either end of my scarf in his hands. Pulling me toward him, he says quietly, "How about if we go for kiss number three."

Kiss number three turns into kiss number four, number five, and so on. After kiss number eleven, he pulls back. "I think I'm going to run out of room in my journal."

I dash back into the gift shop and grab a notebook with candy canes and reindeer on the front. Looking around, I whisper, "Don't worry, Santa, I'm good for it. I'll settle up later."

After I walk back into Santa's workshop, I hand the notebook to Max. "Merry Christmas. I know this isn't as nice as your leather-bound diary—"

"Journal," Max interrupts me.

"Diary, journal, whatever." I put my arms around his waist. "Now, let's get to work filling up the pages."

EPILOGUE – MAX

"Why is mommy crying?" Lila tugs on the bottom of my coat. "Is she sad?"

"No, those are her happy tears. She has happy memories of this place." I ruffle my daughter's hair, then look over at the display of candy by the entrance to Santa's workshop. Zoe is clutching a large candy cane in one hand, and dabbing her eyes with the other. I scoop Lila up in my arms. "This is the third time mommy and I have been here. The first time was for work, then we came back a year later and I proposed to mommy."

Lila counts the fingers on her right hand. "One, two, three—" When she reaches her ring finger, she squeals. "Four. That's how old I am, daddy!"

"You're a big girl, aren't you?" I gently squeeze her pinkie. "What comes after four?"

She giggles. "Five, silly."

"That's right. Mommy and I got married five years ago."

"Did you get married in Santa's Village?" Lila asks.

"No, we got married in Australia. This is the first time mommy and I have been back to Santa's Village since I proposed," I say.

Lila's eyes light up at the mention of Australia. "Kangaroos!"

"What's this about kangaroos?" Zoe asks as she walks toward us. My heart melts at the sight of my wife and daughter together. Lila has her mother's blonde hair and sparkling blue eyes, but she inherited my curls. While my curly hair always looks unruly, Lila's ringlets are adorable. Just like she is.

"I want to see a kangaroo," Lila says.

"It's a little cold here for kangaroos, sweetie," Zoe says, kissing Lila's cheek. "I don't think they like to hop around in the snow. How about if we go see the reindeer after lunch instead?"

Zoe puts her hands on either side of her head, pretending they're antlers. Lila grins, then mimics her mother. "Rudolph," she shouts repeatedly at the top of her lungs. The other parents waiting to see Santa give us an understanding smile, especially those whose kids have taken up their own Rudolph chant.

We eventually manage to get Lila to lower her voice, explaining that the reindeer are probably napping. "We don't want to wake them up, do we?" Zoe asks. "It's Christmas Eve. They have a long night ahead of them delivering presents to boys and girls around the world."

As we near the front of the line, one of Santa's elves approaches, a clipboard in hand. She cocks her head to one side and stares at me. "You look familiar. Were you the guy who stole Santa's suit a few years ago?"

"I think Santa might have put you on his naughty list that year," Zoe says with a teasing tone to her voice.

Lila pipes up. "You shouldn't steal, daddy."

"I like to think of it as 'borrowed,'" I say. "And it was for a good cause. Dressing up as Santa was what clinched the deal for your mommy. That dapper red suit was why she said yes when I popped the question."

Zoe squeezes my arm. "I would have said yes no matter how you were dressed. Well, maybe not as a hedgehog though."

The elf smiles. "I think it was sweet. Definitely memorable." After taking down our information, she ushers us in to see Santa Claus. Lila squirms out of my arms and rushes over, talking a mile a minute about what a good girl she was this year, and could Santa please bring her a kangaroo. Or a reindeer. Or both.

Santa listens patiently, letting out a "Ho, ho, ho" from time to time.

When our turn is over, we point Lila in the direction of the candy display. "You can pick out one piece of candy," Zoe says.

Lila claps her hands together. "I want a candy cane."

"Like mother, like daughter," I say.

While she studies her candy cane options, I put my arm around my wife and whisper, "Why don't I sneak back to the gift shop this evening and pick up a stuffed reindeer for Lila?"

Zoe nods. "Better see if they have a stuffed kangaroo too."

We wait patiently while Lila compares the various kinds of candy canes. When

I Saw Mommy Kissing Santa Claus starts playing over the speakers, Zoe looks at me and grins. "Maybe you should borrow that red suit again."

I pull her toward me. "I don't need to dress up as Santa Claus to kiss you, do I?"

Zoe stands on her tiptoes and lightly brushes her lips against mine. "No, you don't. But you do make a cute Santa. And you're going to make an even cuter father . . . " She smiles mysteriously at me as her voice trails off.

I furrow my brow. "Huh? I'm already a father."

"What I was going to say was you're going to be a cute father of two."

My eyes widen as she lightly touches her belly. "You mean we're having another baby?"

"I was going to tell you tomorrow on Christmas Day, but I couldn't wait," Zoe says, her eyes shining with excitement. "Merry Christmas!"

I tuck a lock of Zoe's hair behind her ear. "This is the best Christmas present ever."

Lila rushes over, clutching a candy cane in her hand. "What did mommy give you? Is it a hedgehog?"

As Zoe breaks into laughter, I say, "No, it's something much cuter than a hedgehog."

"Nothing's cuter than a hedgehog," Lila says.

"Trust me, this is going to be way cuter than a hedgehog." I pick my daughter up, then gaze at my gorgeous wife. Just when I think Christmas can't get better, it does.

ABOUT THE AUTHOR

Ellen Jacobson is a chocolate obsessed cat lover who writes cozy mysteries and romantic comedies. After working in Scotland and New Zealand for several years, she returned to the States, lived aboard a sailboat, traveled around in a tiny camper, and is now settled in a small town in northern Oregon with her husband and an imaginary cat named Simon.

Find out more at
ellenjacobsonauthor.com

ALSO BY ELLEN JACOBSON

Smitten with Travel Romantic Comedies

Smitten with Ravioli
Smitten with Croissants
Smitten with Strudel
Smitten with Candy Canes
Smitten with Baklava

Mollie McGhie Cozy Sailing Mysteries

Robbery at the Roller Derby
Murder at the Marina
Bodies in the Boatyard
Poisoned by the Pier
Buried by the Beach
Dead in the Dinghy
Shooting by the Sea
Overboard on the Ocean
Murder aboard the Mistletoe

North Dakota Library Mysteries

Planning for Murder

Printed in the USA
CPSIA information can be obtained
at www.ICGtesting.com
LVHW041927141123
763965LV00007B/159